2

3

The Two Mommas.

By

John C Burt.

4

PHOTOGRAPHS
COURTESY OF :
    mitchell - gaiser.
    justin - kauffman.
    julien - tondu.
Free Downloads on :
    unsplash.com

There
once was
' The Two
Mommas '.

8

One Momma went by the name of Jackie the Momma Bear and the other 9

Momma
Bear was
known as
Momma Sly.
The two
mommas ...

10

loved
nothing
better than
spending
their days
on a blue as

blue couch in
the middle
of the forest
of rather
large and
very tall and

14

some would say, overgrown green things! But the two .....

15

mommas
did not seem
too worried
about the
overgrown
forest that...

16

was around them ... They just loved spending time together.

When the two ...... mommas were not on the couch, it did seem to

be rather
sad ... and
even ....
deserted of
all known
life ....

Momma
Jackie and
Momma Sly
loved the
views of
what was ...

going on in
the forest
around
them that
the couch
gave them!

24

25

But a test of their friendship was coming? ... They soon ..

would have
to choose a
new couch,
as the old
blue couch
was wearing

out.... The old blue as blue couch had seen better days!

Momma

Jackie wanted a lovely, old as old couch colored yellow ......

Momma Sly
thought you
could not go
past a lovely
old brown
mountain's..

couch ...
Like the one
the rich
folks from
the big cities
had in their

cabins in the
so - called
wilderness
of the Rocky
Mountains...
Momma Sly..

could just imagine herself and Momma Bear Jackie sipping on..

their tea in
the wilds of
the
wilderness
on the old
brown couch!

In the end
the two
Mommas,
the Momma
Bear's kept
the old blue
couch !

40

41

42

44

CPSIA information can be obtained
at www.ICGtesting.com
Printed in the USA
LVHW020429200520
656044LV00024B/1138